Noddy's
Super Busy Day

This edition published by

📖HarperEntertainment

A Division of HarperCollins*Publishers*

It was a busy day in Toyland. Everybody had lots of things to do, but Noddy had more to do than anybody.
He hurried through the market as fast as he could.

"Are you very busy, Noddy?" asked Dinah Doll.

"Yes," replied Noddy. "I have to pick up some fish for Miss Pink Cat's dinner party and then get some hay for the animals at Mr. Noah's ark."

"Do you have time to pick up a box for me at the station?" Dinah Doll asked. "It's my new kitchen stool."

"Sure," said Noddy.

When Noddy arrived at the station, Bert Monkey was standing at the entrance trying to hide something behind his back.

"Hello, Bert Monkey!" cried Noddy. "Have you seen a box?"

"No, I don't think so," replied Bert Monkey nervously.

"What's that behind your back?" asked Noddy suspiciously.
"Um . . . I'm sure it's not a box," said Bert.
"Bert Monkey! Step aside!" ordered Noddy.

Bert Monkey stepped aside and turned around so that his tail covered Noddy's eyes.

"Stop that, you silly tail," exclaimed Noddy, pushing the tail away.

Noddy went up to the box and looked at it. It was for Dinah Doll.

"If you put that box in your car, there won't be any room for me and I need a ride!" wailed Bert Monkey.

"There will be room for you, Bert," Noddy told him, "if you help me carry the box to my car and hold it very tightly as I drive."

As Noddy's car puttered down the road, Bert's tail curled itself around Noddy's shoulder and then knocked Noddy's hat over his eyes.

"Help!" cried Noddy. "I can't see!"

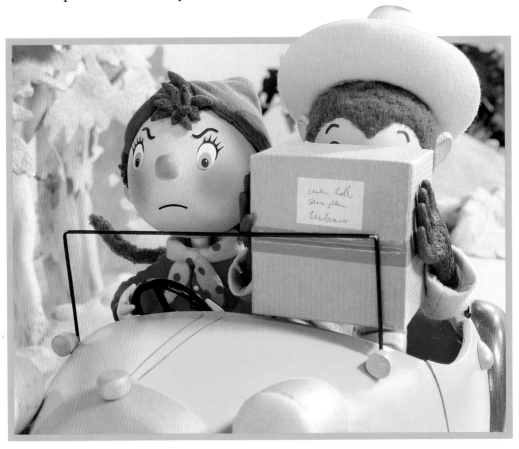

The car swerved, stopping so suddenly that the box flew out of Bert's hands. It sailed up into the air and landed on the ground with a crash.

"Look! Dinah's stool is broken!" Noddy cried. "Your tail is so naughty!"

Soon after Noddy had taken the stool home to fix it, Master Tubby stopped by.

"I'm very good at woodwork," he said.

"If you fix this stool for me," said Noddy, "I'll go and get you some lemonade."

But when Noddy came back he found that Master Tubby had put the stool together all wrong.

"What did you do?" cried Noddy. "You've ruined Dinah Doll's stool!"

"No, I didn't," said Master Tubby. "This is far more interesting than a boring old stool!"

"I'll just have to forget about the stool for now," Noddy grumbled. "I've got too many other errands to do."

A few minutes later, Noddy arrived at the harbor.

"I'm here to pick up a special order for Miss Pink Cat," he told Sammy Sailor.

"I've got it right here, Noddy," said Sammy, handing him a package.

Noddy smiled. "At least something has gone right today," he said.

When Noddy was halfway down the road, he began to smell something horrible.

"Ugh!" he said to himself. "It's coming from the package Sammy Sailor gave to me."

Noddy stopped his car and opened the package. Inside were some old fish bones.

"These yucky bones can't be Miss Pink Cat's package!" he cried in disgust. "But I can't go back now. I'll be too late to pick up the hay from the farm!"

At the farm, smoke was billowing out of the barn. Mr. and Mrs. Straw were rushing to and from the duck pond with buckets of water.

"Hurry, Mrs. Straw!" puffed Mr. Straw. "We need more water to put out this fire!"

Noddy stared, horrified.

"We've got a fire in our barn," explained Mrs. Straw.

"I'll call the fire engine!" cried Noddy.

"We did," said Mrs. Straw, "but it hasn't shown up yet."

"I've got an idea," said Noddy. "I'll go get the fire engine myself."

Noddy drove off and soon found Mr. Sparks and his fire engine on the side of the road.

"Quick!" Noddy called out. "Your fire engine is needed at the farm!"

"I wish I could help," said Mr. Sparks miserably. "But I can't get this old truck to move."

"Leave everything to me, Mr. Sparks!" Noddy exclaimed.

Noddy tied his car and the fire engine together with a strong piece of rope. Then Noddy's little car towed the fire engine to the farm, with its bell ringing the whole way.

When they reached the farm, Mr. Sparks flew into action.
"Make way!" he shouted, as he rushed toward the barn with
his fire hose.

"Good work, Noddy!" cheered Mrs. Straw. "But what's that awful smell?"

Noddy told her all about the package of fish bones he'd picked up from Sammy Sailor.

"Our pigs would love those old bones," said Mrs. Straw. "You can leave them with us."

"The fire's out," said Mr. Sparks, "but I had to soak the rest of the hay in the barn to make sure that it won't catch on fire again."

"I'm sorry, Noddy," said Mr. Straw. "You won't be able to take that hay to the ark, after all."

"Oh, no," said Noddy. "All my errands have gone wrong today."

"Don't worry," said Mrs. Straw. "We can give you some hay from our horse's stable."

"Yes," said Mr. Straw. "I'm sure he won't mind."

When Noddy arrived at the ark with hay for the animals, Mrs. Noah was so happy she gave him fifty cents for his trouble.

"Don't worry about Miss Pink Cat's fish," she said. "Our sea lions caught extra fish today. You may take a few."

"Really?" Noddy asked with delight.

Mr. Noah threw the fish down to Noddy one by one.
"Here you go, Noddy," he cried. "Catch!"

Noddy giggled and caught the fish in his hat.
"Thank you very much, Mr. Noah!" he shouted back.

Noddy drove straight to Miss Pink Cat's house.

"Hello, Miss Pink Cat!" he called out cheerfully. "I've brought your fish."

"In another minute you would have been late, Noddy, and I would have been very angry," said Miss Pink Cat.

But Miss Pink Cat wasn't angry now. She took the fish and handed Noddy a quarter. Suddenly Noddy noticed a yellow stool at Miss Pink Cat's feet.

"Are you throwing that out?" he asked.

"Yes," said Miss Pink Cat.

"Maybe I could take it," suggested Noddy.

"Why not?" she replied.

Noddy found Dinah Doll at the café having some ice cream.
"I've got your stool," he told her.
"Wow!" said Dinah Doll. "It's very bright, isn't it?"

"Don't you like it?" asked Noddy.
"I love it," said Dinah Doll.
Noddy was thrilled he could make his friend so happy.

"Have you got time for some ice cream?" asked Dinah Doll.

"Yes," said Noddy, as he leaned back in his chair. "I'm not doing anything else today!"

"Nothing at all?" asked Dinah Doll in surprise.

"Well, if I don't do anything, nothing can go wrong," Noddy said happily. "Right?"

More delightful Noddy books to read and learn from

Noddy and the Great Cake Bake-Off
Learn the Alphabet with Noddy
Learn to Count with Noddy

Noddy's Super Busy Day
First published in 1995 by BBC Children's Books
Copyright © 1999 by HarperCollins Publishers.

Photographs by Joe Dembinski.
Text, design, and photographs copyright © Enid Blyton Limited and BBC Worldwide Limited.
Cover designed by Susan Sanguily.

Based on the television series, *Noddy*, a BBC Worldwide Ltd/Enid Blyton Ltd/
Catalyst Entertainment Inc. co-production. Original animated series produced
by Cosgrove Hall Films, based on the books by Enid Blyton.

ISBN: 0-06-102015-X
HarperCollins®, ☕®, and HarperEntertainment™ are trademarks of
HarperCollins Publishers Inc.
First U.S. printing: 1999
Printed in China
Visit HarperEntertainment on the World Wide Web at http://www.harpercollins.com